Charles A. Higgins

Las Vegas Hot Springs and Vicinity

Charles A. Higgins

Las Vegas Hot Springs and Vicinity

ISBN/EAN: 9783742810267

Manufactured in Europe, USA, Canada, Australia, Japa

Cover: Foto ©Andreas Hilbeck / pixelio.de

Manufactured and distributed by brebook publishing software
(www.brebook.com)

Charles A. Higgins

Las Vegas Hot Springs and Vicinity

Las Vegas Hot Springs

and Vicinity.

By C. A. Higgins.

Issued by the
Passenger Department Santa Fe Route.
August, 1898.

CONTENTS.

I.

∴

Something about Climate, with reference to New
Mexico in general and Las Vegas Hot Springs
in particular. = = = = = = = =

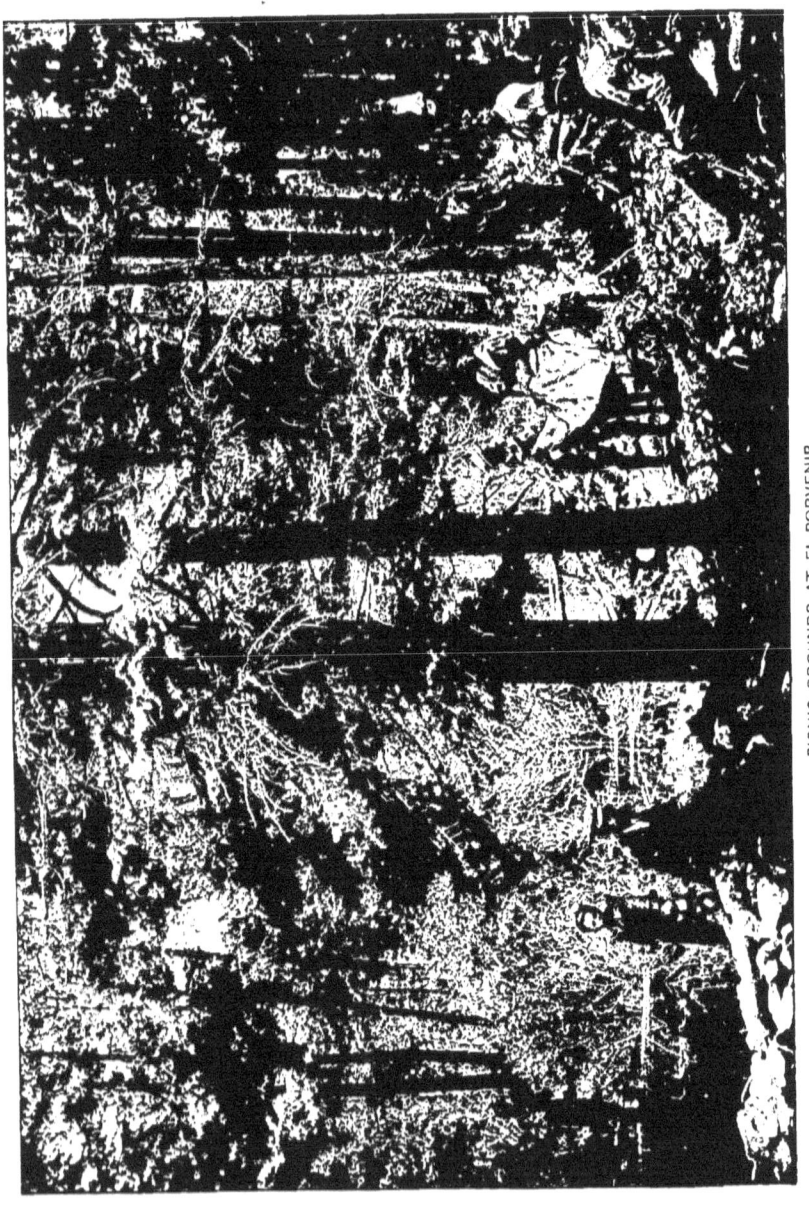

PICNIC GROUNDS AT EL PORVENIR.

N point of latitude New Mexico is southern, just as in point of longitude it is western, for it lies wholly below the 37th parallel and extends southerly beyond the northern line of every one of the Gulf States except Florida.

Is it, then, a land of relaxing winters and torrid summers? By no means. In imagining an untried climate in southern latitudes it is a common error to overlook two very important factors. Elevation above sea-level is the first; humidity, or its absence, is the second. With regard to the first, it should be remembered that an elevation of approximately 800 feet above any given level is climatically equivalent to a degree of latitude; that is to say, an elevation of from 5,600 to 7,000 feet above sea-level on the 36th parallel should, other things being equal, be of the same temperature with sea-level between the 42d and 44th degrees of north latitude. Now, 5,600 feet is the exact mean elevation of the entire Territory of New Mexico; thirty-six degrees is the approximate latitude of Las Vegas Hot Springs, and 7,000 feet its altitude.* On the other hand, all the New England seaside summer resorts, from Bar Harbor to Newport, lie between the 42d and 44th parallels.

You see the point of the comparison: the climate of Las Vegas Hot Springs would be practically the same as that of the New England coast resorts, provided other things were equal.

---

*Actually 6,767.

7

But other things are not equal. There is an enormous difference in favor of New Mexico, due to the almost entire absence of humidity from the atmosphere. It is a country of sparse rainfall, and while it has several important rivers and many small scattered streams, the fact that in agriculture it is almost wholly dependent upon irrigation shows a decided lack of disseminated moisture. The reports of the United States Signal Service contain statistics showing the humidity of most localities throughout the country, and from those reports the following figures are taken:

New England 73%, Middle Atlantic States 74%, South Atlantic States 79%, Ohio Valley and Tennessee 73%, Florida 75%, New York City 72%, San Francisco 76%, New Orleans 79%, Territory of New Mexico 29% to 43%, according to locality.

The contrast presented by these figures is still more strongly marked when it is remembered that by humidity is meant only the amount of *invisible* moisture in the air. The frequent visitations of rain and fog to which the seaside localities named are subjected make the amount of actual atmospheric moisture much greater there, while New Mexico has but little rain and never knew a fog.

The area of the territory is 122,444 square miles, whose mean altitude, as already stated, is 5,600 feet. One-fiftieth of that area rises above 10,000 feet, and it possesses several mountain peaks at least 13,000 feet high. This pronounced altitude of an entire territory, averaging

8

nearly as high as the famous crest of New England's giant, Mount Washington, would certainly be characterized by extreme cold in winter were it not, first, for its southerly latitude, and secondly, for the extraordinary dryness of the air. In point of fact, the combination of these three factors results in a temperate climate whose equability is but little affected by summer or winter solstice.

There is hardly a day in the year when the most sensitive invalids may not be out of doors with impunity, nor is there any season when the infirm may not and do not make excursions among the picturesque hills and inviting cañons, and picnic on the ground. In midsummer the rays of the sun are ardent, but never harmful. No one was ever overheated in New Mexico by work or exercise in the sun ; and in the shade, and at night, it is always cool, for the dry, pure air contains nothing that can be heated. So, in winter, while nights are often cool, they never approach the Eastern experience of winter weather, and with the rising of the sun the temperate warmth returns. Snow buries the distant lofty ranges, and in the night, at rare intervals, falls lightly upon the lower levels, but never remains there save for a day or two in patches among the cañon shades.

GOVERNOR'S PALACE AT SANTA FE.

9

One hundred and eighty-seven days of unclouded sky, one hundred and thirty-nine days when sunshine predominates, and thirty-nine cloudy days make up the average year in New Mexico, and of the thirty-nine days that are cloudy there is hardly one on which the sun does not shine at least a part of the time. On account of this preponderance of clear sky the territory has long been known as The Land of Sunshine. How it can be a land of sunshine in southern latitudes and be free from oppressive summer heat, and how it can lie at an altitude equal to that of the White Mountains and be free from severe winter cold, should now be plain.

But what is the average summer and winter temperature? Now, of all the irresponsible combinations known to numbers, the most abandoned is probably the average; and of all averages the mean temperature of a given locality is, without any doubt, the most barren of information. Imagine, if you please, a country whose temperature is uniformly in summer 61°, and in winter 59°; and another whose summer and winter temperatures are respectively 100° and 20°. The average

CAMPING OUT ON THE GALLINAS.

temperature of each country is 60°, yet the one where the thermometer blisters for six months and congeals the rest of the time is represented by the same figure as the other where there is a variation of only 2° in all the year.

The record of five years' observations at Las Vegas Hot Springs gave the following mean temperatures:

January 41.0, February 49.0, March 56.0, April 58.0, May 61.4, June 71.4, July 74.0, August 71.9, September 65.0, October 55.4, November 53.7, December 52.0, or a mean annual temperature of 59.07. What this record cannot communicate is the fact that the citizen of New Mexico has his cold winter weather at night, when he sits by the fire or lies in bed under an extra blanket; while by day he hardly knows the use of an overcoat. It does not communicate the fact that in midsummer the blanket is still in demand, but the heat of noonday is never distressful.

In the East the mean annual temperature is an averaging of violent extremes of heat and cold. In New Mexico it represents the *habitual* rather than the *average*.

11

CAÑON ABOVE LAS VEGAS HOT SPRINGS.

II.

. . .

A Sanatorium for the Sick, a Recuperating=place
for the Overworked, and a Pleasurable Resort
for the rest of Mankind. ≈ ≈ ≈ ≈ ≈

THE MONTEZUMA, LAS VEGAS HOT SPRINGS.

T happens that there is scarce another known climate so absolutely friendly to man and so valuable an ally against the innumerable forms of disease that lour upon him all the way from the cradle to the grave. Its equability at a comfortable temperature, its pure air, free from humidity and rarefied by altitude, and its almost unclouded sun, render New Mexico the most desirable resort in the world for those who are afflicted with any form of lung or throat disease; and as such it is rapidly being adopted by the medical fraternity, not only in the United States but in several countries abroad. It is a fact that New Mexico numbers among its energetic and prosperous citizens hundreds who, leaving their Eastern or Northern homes a few years ago with no better hope than to prolong by a few months a life apparently doomed to speedy termination by the scourge of our time, consumption, have there regained perfect health and the promise of a long and happy existence. And many others annually desert the harsher regions and repair to New Mexico at the approach of winter to preserve their lives. It is certain that consumption can be arrested, and even permanently cured, by residence there, if the change be made in time. And the climate that can not only withstand but conquer so terrible an adversary is a match likewise for

VIEW FROM THE MONTEZUMA BALCONY.

a long array of other less formidable human ailments. Are you aware for how few localities in the whole world such a sweeping claim can be made without violation of the truth? Do you know that the complications of disease find some fatal flaw in nearly every variety of climate? Even New Mexico makes one exception in welcoming the sick. High altitudes are commonly regarded as aggravating to pronounced heart disease, and sufferers from that malady in an advanced stage are not advised to go there for relief; but every other class of invalid may confidently anticipate the most kindly treatment, for those ailments which the soft ministrations of climate alone cannot wholly obviate yield when such ministrations are supplemented by the medicinal virtues of the Springs, to specific mention of which at last we are come.

Half a dozen miles northwest from the old town of Las Vegas they bubble out of the hillside, some forty of them, varying in temperature from ice-cold to boiling-hot, but most of them ranging from 110° to 140° Fahrenheit.

How long their curative properties have been known to man it is idle to speculate, for the region has been peopled for many centuries, perhaps for thousands of years; but their fame among Mexicans and Indians led to the establishment there of a frontier United States army hospital nearly fifty years ago, while yet the

NEW MEXICAN FRUITS.

northern and western bounds of Texas were the Arkansas River and the Rio Grande, and all west of the Rio Grande and south of Oregon was Spanish dominion, and the wilderness had been penetrated by very few of Anglo-Saxon race. Since that time numberless cases of nearly every form of disease susceptible of mitigation have been either entirely cured or greatly alleviated by the liberal use of these spring waters in drinking and bathing, aided by the health-restoring influences of the climate.

While a chemical analysis has no particular value for the average unprofessional reader, it is a certificate of character to such as understand its meaning. The waters of Las Vegas Hot Springs, therefore, have been subjected to careful test by Dr. Walter S. Haines, Professor of Chemistry, Rush Medical College, who states that in many respects they resemble in chemical com-

position the waters of the famous hot springs of Teplitz and Karlsbad, and finds them to contain special ingredients in the amounts set down below, for every standard gallon :

Carbonate of Calcium .... 0.89 grains.
Carbonate of Magnesium.................... 0.15 "
Carbonate of Sodium .... 8.38 "
Carbonate of Potassium .... 0.28 "
Sulphate of Sodium .... 3.35 "
Chloride of Sodium..........................14.68 "
Silica...................................... 3.50 "
Alumina .. .. 0.10 "
Volatile and Organic Matter .... 0.32 "
Carbonate of Lithium .... Traces.
Bromide of Sodium......................... Trace.

TOTAL.................... 31.65 grains.

DINING ROOM, THE MONTEZUMA.

Ask your family physician whether or not hot natural
spring water so charged with chemicals should possess
remedial qualities. He will tell you that it belongs to
the class termed Alkaline-Saline, and is beneficial in
cases of acute and chronic rheumatism, gout, blood-
poisoning, diseases of the skin, glandular and scrofulous
diseases, mental exhaustion, debility, spinal troubles,
nervous affections, dyspepsia, hay fever, asthma, catarrh,

and a long list of other maladies
which for want of space must be
compressed into *et cetera, et cetera*.
The lithia and sulphur elements
which predominate in some of the
springs are of special medicinal
value.

A combination of climate and
mineral water exists at Las Vegas
Hot Springs which will effectually
rout almost any curable disease.
The invalid who can sit in that sunshine and breathe that air; can drink
that water, bathe in the flow of it, steam
in the vapor of it, lie packed in the mud of
it, and hold fast to his disease through it all, has never
yet been met with. Even imaginary ailments give way
before forces so potent for good.

No one who has taken a Turkish bath ever again
flatters himself he is next door to godliness after a common ablution with soap and water; and just as the
Turkish bath searches out and removes unsuspected ex-
ternal accumulations of foreign matter, so do repeated
draughts of and baths in these hot medicated waters,
piped directly from their hillside environment with
almost no loss of temperature, wash the entire system
free from its impurities and leave the body clean. A
favorite bath here
is administered
by immersion in
peat mud. It is
recommended for
disorders of the
blood.

IN THE MEXICAN QUARTER.

Is not that, then, a favored spot, where healing waters gush forth in unstinted flow, amid surroundings which, even were there no medicinal fountains, would still be unrivaled in the possession of recuperative elements?

And when to these are added vistas of grass-grown meadows between the notches of hills set thick with pine and fir, watered by a stream that flows out from steep rocky walls into winding courses beneath the shade of willow and alder and aspen and maple, idling here and there in transparent pools to have a word with the trout; cañons penetrating the mountain sides, overhung by precipices faced with tree and crag; lofty lookouts and deep secret dells, and far glimpses of purple-shadowed ranges knocking their heads against the distant sky; must not such a spot be worth going far to see and know?

Well, that is Las Vegas Hot Springs, only with a greater diversity of beauty and a subtler charm than so brief a description can convey. Nature did not design it for the sick alone, although for them she made particular provision; the tourist who desires a new sensation; the student of the ruins of antiquity; the dreamer who delights in mementos and suggestions of a romantic and irrecoverable past; the lover of nature who prizes imperishable memories of exalted scenic beauty; the sportsman, devotee of the rod and gun; the man of business

THE BATH HOUSE.

who seeks relief from harassing cares in a retirement at once secluded and invigorating ; and the vast general public that appreciates the delights and benefits of an occasional sojourn in some favored spot where the climate is mild, the sunshine constant and the air inspiring, and where rest, health and profitable pleasures are combined ;— these, equally with the invalid in quest of surroundings whose medicinal virtues shall restore his vanished health, are welcome guests. They will find at Las Vegas Hot Springs not only the natural attractions that have been described and suggested, but a crowning provision for their comfort and happiness in the luxurious and perfectly appointed Montezuma, — the only thing that was wanting, after the completion of the railroad, to place this ideal sanatorium at the service of all mankind. The Montezuma is a surprise and delight to visitors, no matter what they may have been led to expect before going to the Springs, for it is not easy to believe in the actual existence of a structure so extensive and magnificent, so complete and modern in every particular, nestled against the side of a cañon far from the accustomed home of lavish expenditure. The dream of a genie slumbering amid his treasures: that is The Montezuma.

In this four-story stone edifice,

with its numerous apartments, there is ample accommodation for several hundred guests, while the spacious sunny verandas (fifteen feet in width, a tenth of a mile in length) afford abundant room for a multitude by day or night. Steam heat, electric lights and all other modern conveniences are provided. The baths are close at hand, with every facility and every modern method of application, under the direction of specially trained attendants, and a competent physician. The bath house is a commodious structure, fitted up with all necessary appliances. There is a peat bed here. An ample house has been erected in connection with the bath department, where the peat is employed in the shape of baths, being combined with the hot mineral waters. These baths are especially valuable in skin, blood, liver, kidney, rheumatic and nervous affections, and are a real delight, much pleasure being afforded one who indulges in them. The natatorium is nine feet deep and fifty-four feet long. It is filled with hot spring water, and is for the entertainment of guests. Other conveniences consist of numerous cottages and annexes, a hospital, post office, railroad depot, schoolhouse and telegraph and express office. There is also the Mountain House, closely adjacent, with sun parlor attached; this is a substantial stone

THE FOUNTAIN, LAS VEGAS HOT SPRINGS.

structure of sixty rooms. Car-
riage and saddle horses, ponies,
burros and a variety of convey-
ances are at the disposal of
those who wish to penetrate
the mountain solitudes. Guides
also are provided when desired.
Guests bringing children may
send them to school here.

OFFICE FIREPLACE.

The outdoor treatment is as
much of a feature here as that given under cover, great
stress being laid upon the remedial value of pure air and
sunshine. Some patients prefer to sleep out of doors
at night, and they experience benefit from the practice.
Others spend many hours daily in the open air.

There are trout for fishermen ; quail, ducks and
geese abound, and larger game may be found in the
forest. Decayed monuments of prehistoric peoples exist
for the beguilement of the archæologist and historian.
Music, dancing, billiards and bowling are provided for
the lovers of such pleasures, the large entertainment
hall being a feature of the place. An air of quiet rest
pervades the scene, and the invalid is undisturbed by the
activities of his more robust fellows. The encompassing
foothills, which protect the place from severe winds, are
an important factor in promoting restfulness. No sand
storms occur at Las Vegas Hot Springs, and there are no
dusty streets to irritate the throat. Pine, piñon, cedar
and spruce trees grow abundantly, filling the air with
balsamic odors. And this resort possesses certain nega-
tive virtues. It has no malaria ; hay fever is unknown ;
epidemics of acute intestinal diseases never occur ; there
are no hot nights and no sultry days.

23

Neither need one contemplate from afar the possible fatigue of a journey. Las Vegas Hot Springs is less than two days' ride by rail from Chicago and St. Louis, and trains carrying palace sleeping cars and reclining chair cars pass Las Vegas daily. Round-trip tickets to Las Vegas Hot Springs at greatly reduced rates may be

BIRD'S-EYE VIEW OF THE MONTEZUMA,

purchased—particulars obtainable of any Santa Fe Route agent.

Dr. Wm. Curtiss Bailey, physician in charge, has provided a system of treatment, administered by skilled nurses and other attendants, calculated to give Las

Vegas Hot Springs high rank as a sanatorium. Those desiring advice as to the adaptability of the climate and waters and of the treatment to individual cases are invited to confer with him freely by mail, addressing him at The Montezuma. Business communications may be addressed to W. G. Greenleaf, manager.

BATH HOUSE AND SURROUNDINGS.

One unacquainted with the forward strides made by New Mexico along the line of material comforts may imagine that The Montezuma bill of fare is a restricted one. Be assured then, that nothing is lacking at The Montezuma which the most fastidious appetite might hunger for. All the staples and luxuries are furnished in their season. A near-by farm, belonging to the establishment, contributes choice home-grown fruits and vegetables of a quality and variety unsurpassed in the Southwest. The Montezuma herd supplies the very best of pure milk, thick cream and yellow butter, and the juiciest meats are brought from adjacent stock ranges. These are cooked and served in the highest style of the culinary art. There is also a flock of forty goats, whose milk is served regularly at table, free of charge, to those who desire it.

The rates at The Montezuma are $2.50 to $4.00 by the day, and $14.00, $16.00, $17.50 and $21.00 by the week. Where two persons occupy a single room a discount of fifty cents each is made from daily rates, or $1.00 each from weekly rates. If three occupy the same room, the weekly rate is reduced $2.00 each. Medical attendance is extra. Special rates are granted parties of three or more who remain a considerable time. For patients a weekly rate is made of $16.00 and upwards ; this includes board, room and ordinary medical attendance and nurse care.

The community of Las Vegas Hot Springs is perhaps unique in one particular. The usual sanatorium consists of one or more buildings and is bounded by four walls, within which, as in a sick-room, the business of recuperation is confined. But here is a village, comprising five hundred acres, dedicated to the restoration of health and under perfect sanitary control. The only feature that conforms to the accustomed idea of a sanatorium is the hospital, which is separated from The Montezuma by a sufficient distance to be unobtrusive.

III.

. . .

= = New Mexican Sketches. = =

TROUT POOL, RIO GALLINAS

A BACKWARD VIEW.

OOK out from the open window of your room in The Montezuma, through which a cool, sweet current is gently blowing. Far below, at the foot of the path that winds along green terraces, a fountain plays among the trees and shrubs of the plaza, behind which, as also to the right, rise steep tree-clad slopes, *sierras* cresting an elevation already more than a mile above the sea. To the left the *vegas* stretch away for sixty miles, their undulations softened by distance into an inviting plain of every conceivable shade of green, gilded by the morning sun. Rest, peace, security, everywhere meet the sight. It is a hushed sabbath of beneficent nature, made more impressive by recollection of a time, not long past, when romance and terror lurked beneath the same smiling face of that landscape, then no less inviting, no less fair. And as you gaze you will reflect upon a still older time, when down the mountain side and out over the grassy *vegas*, his eye beholding nearly the precise picture upon which yours dwells, strode an heroic pioneer, a knight in clanking armor, a gigantic figure in romantic annals—the First Invader.

WOMEN OF THE PUEBLOS.

It is easy to fancy yourself face to face with the sixteenth century. You almost look for the print of the knight's heel in the grass. It was yesterday he passed. And there is a legend that if one should journey eastward for many wearisome, hazardous months one would come upon Atlantic shores, but meet no living soul except lost heathen. And to the north and west lies an unexplored land of undetermined bounds, full of allurement and mystery and peril. It is the genius of the true Christian to adventure and win earth from pagan rule. Great will be the reward of endeavor. The entire kingdom, a thousand leagues across the sea, is agog for news of the New World. Already in anticipation its acclamations greet the hungry ear of the warrior who is resolved to plant its banner in the heart of an unclaimed wilderness and bring under the dominion of the Cross unnumbered multitudes of benighted souls.

But the way is hard; graves lie scattered behind; and the soldiers murmur and wonder whose sturdy frame will next succumb to the rigors of the task, whose

voice will next be missed from the camp-fire song.
Yesterday? He stands before you now, that Invader,
his stern, swart face bent uncompromisingly on you,
faint-hearted follower that you are, his extended arm
still northward pointing. "*Forward, for God and
Spain!*" he thunders. But with a sensation of relief
entirely unheroic, you will scramble back to the
extreme rear of the nineteenth century and go to
breakfast instead.

A PUEBLO.

Yet, in spite of the romantic achievements of the
fifteenth and sixteenth centuries, never was there more
miraculous doing on the face of this round world than
in our own time. The soldier in armor threaded a
perilous way over these mountains and across these
upland plains and lifted here the standard of Spain;
and the wilderness closed behind him upon a bedouin
race unconquered and unyielding. The locomotive
came, morning sun of our later day, and the bedouin

31

fled; and the scattering mist revealed the benignant Saxon ruling the land, irresistible and serene. It is well that he is benignant, that Saxon, for he is a terrible man. Or, rather, he is the manifestation of a law of earth that out of the north and east shall come strength and power. The west wind never wafted the fleet of a conqueror, the tropics never threw victorious armies into the upper zones; the shadow of the dominant man advances with the sun, and Boreas is at his back. He built The Montezuma. Yonder, if you seek the contrast, observe the chief commemorative monument of his world-subjugating predecessor — a squat adobe hut, inhabited by a brown-faced, black-eyed, black-haired family, picturesque in appearance, courtly in manner, but insulated, isolated, as foreign to our real American life as if they dwelt beyond the sea. As for the bedouin Indian, you shall seek an example of his prime in vain. Only cowed remnants of him are scattered here and there, disreputably arrayed, dethroned and ridiculous.

And while you are making onset upon an excellent morning meal in the æsthetic dining hall of The Montezuma, the inhabitants of the adobes will be masticating dried kid and chili. The aborigine has apparently schooled himself not to eat, since the pillaging of the Saxon is become for him a thing forever past.

CHURCH OF SAN MIGUEL   32

2

TOUCHING BURROS.

EVERY living creature is respectable in his native environment. Only when translated into foreign surroundings is he wanting in validity. In contemplating an occasional imported specimen of the *burro* in the East it is possible you have never taken him seriously. In New Mexico, then, you will make amends, for you will find him entirely authentic in his own realm.

Unenterprising, fond of his ease, opinionated, and a doubter; that is the *burro* in outline, up to his ears. As for those huge organs, they were evolved to enable him to catch the faintest first whisper of a command to relapse into statuesque inactivity. In point of fact, they serve him even better, for he often chooses to imagine that such mandate has issued from his rider, and arrogant in the possession of his appalling, winglike appendages he stops, absolutely—and, so far as may reasonably be inferred from his manner, forever. It avails nothing with him to argue that you never said it. He droops an ear gratefully, relaxes a hind leg, shifts his equipoise over

upon the remaining tripod, and waits for the end of the world. Only the most emphatic prodding will persuade him to resume his reluctant way. If he should manifest any seeming inclination toward alacrity it will be due to his discovery that you object to traveling in a direction contrary to that in which your destination happens to lie. In the flash of such a divination he is capable of voluntary activity, and will even break into a jog trot for a distance of twenty yards—an entirely unprofitable ebullition of energy, if you are considering your own interests, for his progress is sidelong, radiate, tangential, what you will except onward to the path of your choice.

It is better not to betray a purpose when mounted upon a *burro;* at any rate, no other purpose than that he shall keep in motion. To effect this you will find the best weapon a goad, improvised from a stout stick, whittled to a point. Prod him with this resolutely, vigorously, frantically; prod him unceasingly. You will not offend him. He expects it. He seems to like it. But do not ask him to follow so logical a sequence as a path—above all the right path. Beat about the bush, and the crag, and behave as if you were going nowhere in particular. Tack him, jibe him, ease him off the

34

instant he appears to divine your secret. If your course lies directly to the north, be content with northwest, northeast, and even occasionally south-southwest; and if you find yourself drifting too decidedly into southern latitudes, act as if you were eagerly bound for the tropics; you can fool him.

It is well to change the goad frequently from hand to hand. This not only enables you to bear up longer against fatigue, but doubles the likelihood of finding a vulnerable spot in his callous epidermis. When your strength finally fails you can walk. You can always find your *burro* again when you want him. To be entirely truthful, that is the worst of a *burro*, that you are morally certain to find him where you left him, whether you want to or not, unless you have been absent so long that hunger has forced him to move.

The present writer does not regard himself as generally either an astute or a vindictive person, but it gives him a malicious satisfaction to this day to remember how he avenged himself on his first (and last) *burro*, abandoned in despair on an outward trip some three miles from The Montezuma. Returning, some few hours later, he passed the contentedly waiting creature without a glance of recognition and footed it back to the hotel with a merry heart, alone. Next morning, they said, the *burro* was found behind the stable, limp, despondent, disgusted, his long cheeks bedewed with tears, his air proclaiming the shadowed, misanthropic soul of one who has been betrayed by man and possesses an ineradicable grievance. He had expected to be pushed home.

35

WHERE THE TROUT STREAMS RISE.

3

THE PECOS CHURCH.

ROM the window of the Pullman car, two hours' ride below Las Vegas, may be seen, a few miles away, a strange brown ruin standing like a dismantled castle upon a fortress-like elevation overlooking the surrounding plain. It is one of the Missions founded by Franciscan monks, nobody appears to know exactly when, but doubtless soon after the Spanish invasion, and something like three hundred years ago. On account of its location at the Pecos pueblo it is locally known as the Pecos Church. Abandoned, solitary, forming with the adjacent débris of still more ancient structures the only visible sign and handiwork of man in that lonely valley, it was once the center of a busy throng, and often the scene of savage warfare.

It may be reached by a four-mile drive from the small station Rowe, over that highway of romantic memory, the old *Santa Fe Trail*. Although a valley hemmed in by mountains, the land is elevated some 7,000 feet above the sea. It stretches broadly before the eye, an arable plain, unbroken save by occasional *arroyos* and the single mound that rises nearly in the center, buttressed on three sides by enormous crags, bastions invulnerable to the assault of an enemy, although the hand of man had nothing to do with its building. Upon this natural elevation the ruin stands like a watch-tower, an adobe shell, roofless and desolate, backed by the débris of what was once a pueblo, a tribal Indian home. Stern must have been the necessity that forced a peaceful primitive people like the Pueblos to choose a stronghold for their dwelling place, and doubtless the Franciscan Fathers bowed to the same necessity in building their church upon the crown of that citadel; for though there is

RUINS OF THE PECOS CHURCH.

still discernible an old irrigating ditch in evidence of once fruitful fields and agricultural occupations, in two hours' search you may find upon the surface of the slopes of the mound a double handful of arrow heads, fashioned from flint and jasper and saw-toothed obsidian ; cruel, jagged things, shot by those untamable wild men whose nature is to make relentless war upon every people except their own.

Little is known of the history of the Pecos Church ; nothing whatever that is trustworthy of the origin of the Pueblos, who differ from the roving Indian tribes almost as widely as if they were not Indians at all. Say that they were stragglers who lagged behind in the great southward march of the Toltecs twelve hundred years ago, and no really well-informed person will be likely to dispute you. But the main story of the ruined church is readable upon its crumbling walls. To a peaceful, populous village of those mysterious Pueblo Indians, huddled in their curious apartment houses of adobe and stones upon the summit of this mound, came the old Spanish priests, and preached the gospel ; and for the better preaching they builded a Mission and there dwelt for a space of years with their flock ; and by and by they went away ; and they and their flock are no more.

Inclined to religious rites, to peace and the gentle pursuits of agriculture, the Pecos Indians still were stubborn fighters for their homes and their kin. Their enemies were unable to dislodge them, unless the final removal of the remnant of the tribe some fifty years ago was an ultimate concession to hostility. At any rate they remained long after the priests had departed, and so long as they remained (so the tradition runs), there ceased not from the altar of the church erected to the glory of the Catholic faith a fire, by night or day, a vestal flame, maintained by the Pueblos in expectation of *Montezuma's* return to earth and power.

39

 The demi-gods have
their habitat as surely as
plant or animal species.
Each must be sought
upon his particular
Olympus ; and because
Montezuma is not to
be found within the boundaries of New England,
nor anywhere upon the prairies of the Western States,
one must not therefore deny him in the land of echo-
ing cañons, of desert tracts, of cacti, of lofty altitudes,
and, withal, of abundant verdure, flowers and fruits,
and of pure air and sunshine. Although you may be
justified in hearkening to the tradition of the vestal
flame with mental reservations, and may have a shrewd
notion that the divinity Montezuma is but an apotheo-
sized Aztec emperor fallen heir to the old clothes of
the god of his worship, Quetzalcoatl, you will not
unlikely gain a juster sense of the difficulties of
engrafting the idealism of a higher race upon the
superstitions of a lower. And while you muse by the
walls of the old church and try to picture a rotund,
shaven, tonsured, cowled company of godly men in
such an incongruous setting, three centuries ago, and
then view the tremendous gulf that intervenes between
that time and the day when the stones upon which
you sit were first piled into rude dwellings for man, you
may reflect that the evolution of pagan gods is a very
human thing. As distance is the first essential of a
landscape, so some degree of remoteness in experience
or space or time is necessary to the appreciation of
poetic beauty, and, perhaps, in turn creates it. We
dream of yesterday and tomorrow. Nobody ever wrote

an ode to the noonday sun; it is only his rising and setting that limners paint and poets sing; the day that is gone, and the day that will come. There is no people, no land, so poor in poetry as not to possess a yesterday. Everywhere you will find some tradition of an Odysseus, a Buddha, a Moses. "To every nation," says the Koran, "God hath given a prophet in its own tongue." And in whatsoever manner his own may have received him, time deals liberally with a great man. It will not have him appear quite mortal to the distant view. It swathes him in atmospheric haze that obliterates something of his human outline, and more and more as we recede. Who among living monarchs can be compared to King Solomon? And can another Cleopatra ever live upon this earth? Already Napoleon has become a semi-myth, an almost incredible tradition of demoniac force, an Attila-scourge, withheld only by the interposition of heaven from overrunning the world. And no man, unrebuked, may now whisper that our own first national hero ever laughed in his sleeve upon the consummation of a horse trade. Time would fain have it so, and poetry demands it. Let us therefore forget of Montezuma that, like Homer, he may be a composite hero. Let him have all his halo and at least half a dozen ways of spelling his name. Let him be prince and prophet and redeemer to a mysterious people whose minds cannot grasp our finer symbols of divinity. Let him be the personification of a heathen idea which, stubborn as the Pueblos themselves, still dwells in the cañons of New Mexico.

WE GO A-FISHING.

4

MOUNTAIN TROUT AND QUAIL.

HE Pecos River is one of the best trout streams in the United States. The trout do not attain the size of those in the Rio Grande in the State of Colorado, but in number and voracity they satisfy the greediest carrier of a creel. Rarely weighing less than half a pound, they often tip the scale at over a pound, and two-pounders are not infrequently taken. Four miles beyond the Pecos Church, almost on the river bank and in the heart of the best fishing, is a comfortable ranch-house, where excellent accommodations in the way of meals and lodging may be obtained. Here, also, is the location of a proposed National Park.

For many miles the stream offers the perfection of fly-fishing. Here and there are pools too deep for wading, but the fisherman equipped with hip-boots is seldom forced to the bank. Following the winding shallows, the entire stream may be whipped, left and right, and every lurking-place under projecting shore and bough ex-

plored with a cast of flies. In a delightful three days
upon this river, the writer recalls but two occasions
of even momentary embarrassment to his leader by
bush or branch, and the avidity with which the Pecos
trout rise to a fly, and the determination with which
they resist capture, has rarely been equaled in his
experience.

What manner of soul has he who does not love to
drop a cast across the translucent riffles of a stream

LAKE AT EL PORVENIR.

that chatters endlessly over sand and pebble and
ledge, through glimpses of field and wood and gorge,
under a friendly sky? In every seductive shoal there
lies a tremendous moment of suspense, an absorbing
riddle one never wearies of guessing. The powerful
and somewhat complex charm of fishing is not com-
prehended by those who depreciate the sport. It was
not the size, or number, or greediness of the trout
that made old Walton declare that "other joys are but
toys"; and if the trout imagine they alone make or

44

unmake the fisherman's joy they are a fatuous lot — his main business is with the brooding mother of us all.

There are those who would have us think that the sportsman is a barbarian — that he who can complacently asphyxiate inoffensive fishes and slaughter innocent birds has not attained to perfect civilization — is, in fact, hopelessly below that state of grace. Although New Mexican trout are a comparatively easy prey, the hunter of mountain quail, to be quite candid, is not necessarily so murderous in fact as in appearance. The question of the fate of an uprising quail never outgrows the small dignity of a riddle with many gunners. "Shall I get him?" That is their query. They guess with the right barrel, often guess again with the left, and not infrequently after both guesses find themselves without a pang of conscience — and without the bird.

He who cares to try his hand at mountain quail will find an abundance of two very sprightly varieties of that gamebird in numberless New Mexican localities. The tyro will need all his self-command in the first few encounters. These quail are fleet-footed, and take to their wings reluctantly, preferring at first to attempt escape by running. A sharp pursuit forces them to flight, and as a covey usually numbers scores, and sometimes even hundreds, 'the 'clatter of their simultaneous uprising is extremely disconcerting to inexperienced nerves. Their flight is short, and upon this fact is based the only effectual method of hunting them. One must pursue, and shoot without regard to bagging, until several rapid flushings and repeated salvos have robbed them of confidence in their legs and wings. Then they scatter and lie close. At this juncture only is a dog serviceable, and fair sport may be had without one, as after the birds have been thus bewildered they will lie until the ground has been pretty thoroughly beaten up, and will offer successive singles and doubles in abundance as they are closely approached.

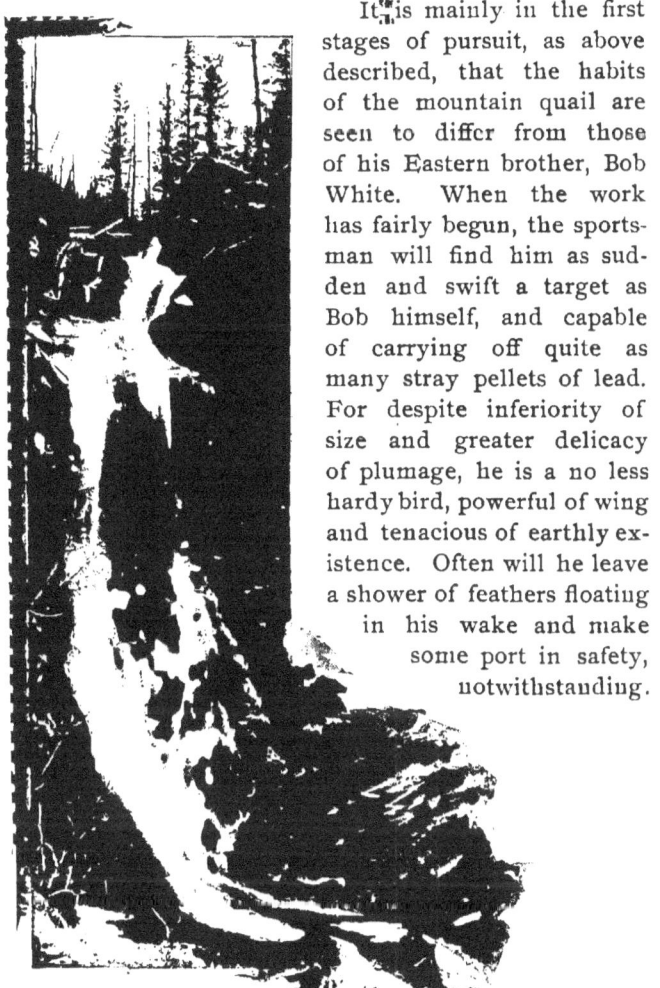

It is mainly in the first stages of pursuit, as above described, that the habits of the mountain quail are seen to differ from those of his Eastern brother, Bob White. When the work has fairly begun, the sportsman will find him as sudden and swift a target as Bob himself, and capable of carrying off quite as many stray pellets of lead. For despite inferiority of size and greater delicacy of plumage, he is a no less hardy bird, powerful of wing and tenacious of earthly existence. Often will he leave a shower of feathers floating in his wake and make some port in safety, notwithstanding.

ANNOUNCEMENT.

✤

This is one of a series of publications, issued by the Santa Fe Route, descriptive of the various health and pleasure resorts along its line in Colorado, New Mexico, Arizona and California.

Copies of the other books will be mailed on application.

www.ingramcontent.com/pod-product-compliance
Lightning Source LLC
Chambersburg PA
CBHW021236260626
47172CB00002B/799